· *mwynhad* ·

SEATTLE

ARIADNE'S EGG

BY CHRYSTAL WING

ARIADNE'S EGG
Copyright © 2001 Chrystal Wing

mwynhad
1615 43 Avenue East #101
Seattle, Washington 98112

www.mwynhad.com

"Ariadne Has a Small Wedding" was previously published in *The Dissident,* Summer, 1997.

Cover painting, *Luna* by Lezli Morgan, used by permission
Author photo by Suzanne Hunt

ISBN 0-9657993-7-9
Library of Congress Catalog Card Number 2001 126168

for Roxie

.

ARIADNE HAS BREAKFAST

Ariadne plucked the foil-covered Pop Up Tarts out of the squat little box. She ripped the foil open and smiled at the two tarts nestling side by side. Into the toaster oven they went. Ariadne waited, hands on hips, toe tapping, as they turned golden under the fierce red bars of the toaster. The smell of strawberry jam wafted on the air. After she had transferred the lovely rectangles to her plate and made herself some tea with milk and wildflower honey, after she had slathered some butter so it melted into the crust, after she had trimmed off the ends that were a little too brown, Ariadne picked up a tart and bit deeply.

Her cat cried in the next room, startled out of a dreamless sleep. The refrigerator hummed. Birds twittered like wind-up toys outside the window. The day began.

ARIADNE GETS DRESSED

Ariadne could not decide what to wear. She put on a Lois Lane suit with a peplum jacket and cloth-covered buttons, then tried a black sequined evening dress with a plunging neckline, then a pair of leather pants and a Grateful Dead T-shirt, then a bikini with appliquéd daisies and thong sandals, then a leopard-print coat with a fox stole collar. She took the final outfit off and stood naked in the middle of the floor. Clothing draped the backs of chairs, the door knob, the bureau top. She hung everything in the closet and crawled into bed, pulling the blanket up over her eyes. She wished that someone would bring her cinnamon toast and tea.

This went on for days or maybe weeks. She would rise from bed knowing exactly what she wanted to wear, but once she was dressed the waistband would feel too tight or the label would scratch her neck. Or worse, she'd look in the mirror and see a little girl decked out in dress-up clothes, lipstick too red and unevenly applied, feet lost in pointy-toed high-heeled shoes. She would give up and burrow back under her blankets.

One night she heard a whispery sound in her closet. She'd had too much sleep lately, so she was wide awake, staring at the ceiling above her bed. Then she heard it, softly, in the moon-lit room: dresses rustling against trousers, blouses sliding sleeves around the waists of skirts, the tiny squeak of a hanger on the metal rod. Ariadne slipped from her bed and tiptoed to the closet door. She pressed her ear to the wood; there was a rush of sound like the wings of birds flapping, and then silence.

She opened the door. The clothes were neat and symmetrical on their hangers. The light of the moon washed out all the colors; silver gray fabric faded to black down at the hems. She was a little afraid of the

4

yawning darkness where the shoes should be. She closed the door.

The next day she got out of bed, wrapped a blanket around her naked self and sat in the chair by the window. Sparrows pecked at the seeds in the birdfeeder. An airplane flew low overhead and shook the house. A maple leaf drifted by. Ariadne pulled the blanket up around her face and sat in the sun like an old woman.

The day passed and she remained by the window. She woke with a start, her head jerking up against the back of the chair. It was late afternoon, past the time that it should be. In her dreams she had remembered a set of small translucent white wings that she kept at the back of her closet. They were part of a costume . . . moth, angel, bumblebee, hummingbird, fairy godmother, dragonfly . . . whatever you wanted it to be. She tied the blanket in a secure knot around her waist and went to find the wings. The hangers screeked as she parted them; the clothes murmured and settled. And there they were, hanging on a hook in the darkest corner. They glittered faintly. Ariadne slipped her arms through the white elastic cords and adjusted them around her shoulders. The wings were light, yet substantial.

It was at this moment that the clothes in the closet went wild. Blouses were unbuttoning and dresses unzipping, sweaters pulling themselves inside out, shoes stepping on each other, trouser legs winding themselves into a knot. There was a riot of colors and textures: red taffeta arguing with polyester pants, an alligator purse snapping at fleece-lined slippers. A silk kimono tried to slip to the back of the closet, only to be snared by a brass-buckled belt and pulled back in.

Ariadne readjusted her wings and stepped back from the closet, closing the door. She left the bedroom and walked down the hallway—her blanket trailing behind her, her wings resting high on her shoulders—to make herself some toast and tea.

ARIADNE VISITS WITH HER MOTHER

Ariadne sat across from her mother at Pizza Heaven, and as they talked Ariadne reached into her ear and pulled out a dry thread of wax. It was flat like dental floss, only wider, and golden. It slid out of her ear like a stopper from a bottle, slow, sensuous, tickling the tiny hairs of the inner ear. She laughed with delight. Her mother was grossed out so she dropped it on the floor. They ate their breadsticks.

The next day Ariadne went to her mother's house to borrow a cup of love. Her mother was talking as Ariadne walked into the kitchen and continued talking throughout the whole visit. Ariadne's ear began to hurt. Then it began to flutter deep inside, like a moth beating its wings. She tipped her head to the side and jumped up and down. Stuff came out: seeds and beads, grains of uncooked rice. Then came a collie puppy, which ran around in circles on the kitchen floor, barking from happiness. Her mother was still talking. Ariadne cupped one hand around her emptied ear, straining to catch her mother's meaning.

ARIADNE'S FRIEND

A letter came for Ariadne in an envelope as yellow as a daffodil. The return address was to a company called Fantasy Friends Inc. On the front of the envelope were stamped the words: ARE YOU A NICE PERSON? DON'T YOU DESERVE A NICE FRIEND? LET US CREATE THE PERFECT FRIEND FOR YOU!

"I'm nice!" said Ariadne, excited that she qualified. She was a little confused by the word CREATE, but decided it was just over-zealous advertising. Inside the envelope there was a personality test. She ran

9

back up to her apartment and sat on the couch to fill in her answers. Some of the questions were:

What is your favorite bird?

What is your favorite dessert?

What is your favorite sound?

What is your favorite board game?

"Hah! This is easy." Ariadne quickly scribbled *parrot pie drums Parcheesi* in the spaces provided. She had to think about her answers to the favorite smell and color, then settled on cinnamon and bright orange. She sent the test back the very same day, being sure to include her $19.95 plus postage in the return envelope.

She tried to imagine the friend they'd pick out for her. Would they call or write? Would they set up a meeting? Her nerves were all aquiver.

At last, the doorbell rang. There, on the doormat, sat a huge cardboard box. Fortunately, it was lighter than it looked, and she managed to squeeze it through the front door and bump it upstairs.

She slit the box open and scooped out a layer of Styrofoam peanuts. At first everything was a colorful jumble. Then, some of the items started to look familiar. She saw a life-sized plaster arm, and some parrot feathers, and a glue gun. She saw a Parcheesi game, a wooden foot with a black and white saddle shoe, and all of the ingredients to make a banana cream pie.

"What can this mean?" said Ariadne. She found a sheet of instructions taped to the inside of the box. Her eyes widened as she skimmed the page, reading: Insert arm into armhole socket A. Glue in place.

"Holy cow!" she said. "It's a lot harder to make a friend than I thought!"

She dedicated herself to a day of manual labor, and soon the living room floor was covered with all of the things she had said were her favorites.

The pink arms looked like they'd come from a mannequin; they were self-consciously graceful, the elbows bent, the hands trying to express an excitement about something just out of reach. The legs were stuffed like the head and the body, but ended at the ankle. This explained the wooden feet wearing saddle shoes and white ankle socks.

In the bottom of the box she found a plastic bag. "The face!" she cried happily. She glued wax lips into place, and they smiled up at her, rosy and full. The eyes were two round chunks of black obsidian. They glittered as she moved them about, trying to get the expression on the face just right. After attaching clam shell ears, she realized that the parrot feathers would serve well as hair. Blue and red and green, she stuck the quills into the soft head until it bristled with bright plumage.

"Aren't you gorgeous," Ariadne said.

She attached the feet to the legs, the legs and arms and head to the body. She propped her friend up in a sitting position on the couch. The head lolled forward and Ariadne tipped it back. She frowned and looked over her remaining materials.

"Oh! I get it." She wiggled a tiny refrigerator with a see-through glass door into a hole in the belly, tucking back in any stray bits of stuffing that escaped. "Don't mind me, Zelda," she said, trying out one of the names that had been floating through her mind.

A miniature tape recorder fit snugly into a hole in the small of Zelda's back. The Parcheesi board she glued to her friend's lap, setting out the game pieces and the dice. Last of all, with a feeling of great ceremony, she affixed two large crepe paper poppies, both of them a brilliant orange color, to her friend's flat chest. They looked quite jaunty there.

Ariadne stepped back to survey her work, and saw that it was good. She had put the left foot on crooked, making Zelda a little pigeon-toed, but that just added to her new friend's charm: the reaching hands, the feathery hair, the clam shell ears that seemed to listen to each and every word that Ariadne said.

What followed was a time of quiet happiness for Ariadne. The two friends sat side by side on the couch and played Parcheesi by the hour, Ariadne moving the pieces for Zelda. When Ariadne was hungry, she took a piece of pie (made from the ingredients provided by Fantasy Friends) out of the refrigerator in Zelda's belly. When she wanted to hear the exciting rhythms of many African drums, she pressed the On button in her friend's lower back. Ariadne was a little disappointed that Zelda was such a sedentary person, but otherwise their friendship flourished. Before going to bed each night, she kissed Zelda on her smiling red lips. They tasted like cinnamon.

One morning, not too long after Zelda's arrival, Ariadne awoke with a feeling that something was missing.

"What is the matter with me?" she said. "Don't I have the perfect friend sitting in the next room?" But still the strange feeling persisted.

She hurried to the living room to reassure herself. Zelda was there on the couch, as always. Ariadne sat down and picked up her friend's hand; the unnaturally pink plaster was cool and unyielding. The crepe paper flowers on Zelda's chest rustled in the breeze coming from an open window.

"Tell me, Zelda . . . " Ariadne hesitated and tightened her grip on Zelda's hand. She took a deep breath. "Tell me, my dearest Zelda, do you love me as much as I love you?"

Zelda's lips smiled and smiled. Why, she smiles like a hostess at a cocktail party, Ariadne thought.

She became uncomfortable with the silence and reached around Zelda to turn on the tape. The deep, throbbing sound of the drums filled the room, intensifying Ariadne's feeling that something was missing from this relationship. She stared down at the delicately formed Parcheesi pieces on the board on Zelda's lap and felt like knocking them to the floor.

"Zelda," she said again, speaking loudly over the drumming. "I don't mean to criticize, but don't you think you could be a little more forthcoming?"

The drums got louder and faster. A feather came loose from Zelda's head and drifted to the floor.

"Well?" Ariadne said impatiently. "Aren't you going to answer me? Do you love me or not?"

She grabbed Zelda by the shoulders and shook her, making her feathered head wobble. The Parcheesi pieces flew to the far corners of the room. "Tell me!"

14

she pleaded, looking into the glittering black eyes. Ariadne was so overwrought, she didn't realize that one of Zelda's arms had come unglued. It slid down onto the Parcheesi board with a thump.

Ariadne jumped back, frightened by her own violence. "What have I done?" she whispered. She fumbled with the arm, trying for several minutes to reattach it. Finally she gave up, and Zelda slumped sideways over the arm of the couch.

Ariadne sat down on the other end of the sofa, and thought for the rest of the day about the nature of friendship. She didn't play Parcheesi, or eat pie, and the drumming she shut off after it started to give her a headache. Her final thought, as the room turned dark and she rose to go to bed without giving Zelda her usual good night kiss, was that she didn't understand friendship at all.

HOW
SPRING
AFFECTS
ARIADNE

Ariadne went out walking, her boots tapping a steady rhythm on the pavement, her pedal pushers chafing gently against her knees. She had had many bad days lately, sitting alone in her living room, and she was determined to get out into the world. The sun was warm. The squirrels were absurdly happy, chasing each other up and down trees. The concrete slabs of the sidewalk were tilted this way and that. She passed a businessman who wore a self-conscious grin, an old woman who talked to herself, a younger woman who carried daffodils.

Ariadne found that she was irrepressibly drawn to the bodies that passed her, first pulled to the right, then to the left, making a gentle zigzag down the sidewalk.

"How strange!" she said.

Another businessman approached her. He swung his leather briefcase and whistled a little tune, but Ariadne looked into his eyes and saw: desolation. Without thinking about it, she began to walk directly towards him, his maroon tie a target in the center of his chest. He looked alarmed. Then for one second his eyes lit up, his body ready for the impact. At the last moment, he jumped out of her way.

"Excuse me!" he said.

"Pardon me," said Ariadne, and walked on. The squirrels cavorted in the trees. She stepped on little pieces of glass on the sidewalk, listening to them crunch under her heavy boots.

"Well, this is worrisome," she said. She thought about what it might mean, this sudden desire to collide with people. The truth was, some part of herself was still on the living room couch with all of the shades drawn.

She heard quick steps behind her and a young woman jogged past, her long braid swinging from side to side. The woman wore bright red shorts and a canary yellow T-shirt, but the stiffness in her shoulders made Ariadne think: sorrow.

"She's on her couch, too," said Ariadne, who then felt like running after the woman and butting her between the shoulderblades, affectionately, like a billy goat. But the woman was gone.

Ariadne continued walking a slightly crooked course through the town, feeling the gravity of each person she passed. She saw wooden benches bolted to the ground and trees puckering with pale green buds. Spring was coming and the world was trying to crack itself open.

A little man with a backpack stood in front of the library. He wore a baseball cap. His small hands caressed the green and yellow hardcover books he carried. He watched the oncoming traffic, waiting patiently for his bus to appear. Ariadne wanted to knock him over like a bowling pin. She hurried past, resisting the impulse. If only he didn't look so alone, she thought. His couch is plaid and the room is dark. The phone on the end table never rings.

She turned a corner and saw someone walking slowly towards her. The woman was all dressed up in high heels and a skirt and blouse. Ariadne was admiring the cut of the narrow skirt (how does she walk in it? she wondered) when she saw that the woman was crying.

"Wow," said Ariadne.

Tears flowed down the woman's cheeks and onto the collar of her yellow silk blouse. A violet was strung through the top buttonhole. Her hair was coming loose from an arrangement of combs on top of her head, and her sobs were soft and insistent, as if she was consoling herself with the sound of her own voice. She walked with her arms wrapped protectively around her belly.

Ariadne was unhinged by this weeping. She was afraid to do what she wanted to do. But the urge was so strong. As the woman approached, Ariadne concentrated on the cracks in the sidewalk to help calm her nerves. When she came abreast, Ariadne swayed, timing it so that she bumped the woman's shoulder gently, yet firmly.

The woman tottered sideways on her high heels. After she regained her balance she stared at Ariadne, wide-eyed and speechless.

"Sorry," said Ariadne. "I couldn't help myself." She gave the woman a tissue. Then she dug around in the pocket of her pedal pushers and found a cough drop; she picked off the lint and gave that to the woman, too.

"The cough drop is mango-flavored," said Ariadne.

The woman looked at the paper-wrapped lozenge in her hand. "Mango," she repeated numbly. She raised the tissue to her face and blew her nose. With a clean corner she dabbed under her eyes.

Ariadne struggled to find some words. "Did you see the grass?" she said. The woman sniffed and wiped her nose again, then looked where Ariadne was pointing. They took in the gorgeously greening blades at their feet.

"It's beautiful," said the woman softly. "Beautiful."

Ariadne smiled at her. The woman looked shy, then smiled back. She lifted the loose hair off her neck and pinned it back in place on top of her head. Ariadne retrieved a fallen comb from the ground. She handed it to the woman.

"Thank you for crying like that," Ariadne said. "So opened up. It makes me hopeful that I'll get off my couch. I've been on it for way too long."

The woman looked confused, and like she thought Ariadne might be a little crazy, but she continued to smile. "That's good," she said.

"Goodbye," said Ariadne. "Take care of yourself."

She walked on, a little more slowly than before, her boots thoughtfully kissing the sidewalk with every step. "Bye!" the woman called out. Ariadne looked back and waved without stopping. The squirrels flicked their tails and chattered. The sun was absurdly bright. "It's spring," she said to herself, and for the first time, she felt it was true.

ARIADNE GOES TO THE CIRCUS

Ariadne unbuttoned her purple overalls and pushed down her lavender underpants. She sat on the toilet. She enjoyed the urgency, then the splashing release of her pee, and finally the zen-like emptiness. A tiny spider crossed the towel rack like a circus performer, testing each step with a delicate leg. It swung from the towel rack down to the bathtub rim, startling Ariadne with its reckless abandon.

"Good for you," she said.

She rested her cheek against the fat roll of toilet paper and waited patiently for the spider's next trick.

ARIADNE GETS A PRESCRIPTION FILLED

The pharmacist looked at the slip of paper Ariadne had just given him. "This is a powerful prescription," he said severely, tapping the paper with a ball point pen. "What exactly is troubling you?"

The pharmacist's counter was so high Ariadne was tempted to rest her chin on it. Chapstick and ear plugs and vitamins A, B, C, D, and E were on display to her left and right. She yearned for vitamin F without knowing why.

"I'm not able to experience abandon," she whispered.

The pharmacist squinted at her over his bifocals. He was a little old man with a big head, wearing a leather vest and a scarlet tie under his white lab coat.

"What's that you say?"

"Abandon," she said louder, blushing and looking around the drugstore.

He slowly nodded his head. "A serious problem . . . but treatable." He turned and searched the shelves, bringing down a big glass jar. The jar was filled with small purple hearts, translucent like cough drops.

"I'll fill this prescription for you, but you have to follow the instructions carefully."

He removed one of the hearts from the jar with tongs and dropped it into a small, clear glass vial of liquid. He capped the vial and stuck a label on the side.

"Take one sip every hour. No more and no less." He took her money and handed her the medicine in a white paper bag.

"How will I know when . . ." Ariadne peeked in the bag nervously. "How will I know when I'm better?"

The pharmacist smiled. "You'll know."

Ariadne left the drugstore and waited at the curb for the light to change. Trucks barreled through the intersection. A bicyclist went by so close she could smell paint fumes on his clothes. The orange hand blinked monotonously on the other side of the street.

Now is as good a time as any, she thought, and took the medicine out of the bag. She held the vial up to the sunlight. The purple heart glimmered, suspended in its clear liquid. She uncapped the vial and took a tiny sip; it tasted sweet but not too sweet. The translucent heart bobbed against her lips as she sipped. When she lowered the vial, her vision blurred for a second and she felt dizzy. She quickly put the cap back on, worried that she'd taken too much.

The orange hand was still blinking across the street. Another truck went by, blowing debris past her feet: a crumpled newspaper, autumn leaves, a candy wrapper, someone's math homework, an empty soda can that clanked and clattered, hitting her toe and bouncing onwards. Ariadne felt the suck of the wind on her body. She staggered a bit to her left, then pulled herself back.

The orange hand finally changed to the little walking person. Before stepping out into the road, she waited a moment to see if the heart medicine would cause any more symptoms. She felt fine, she decided, ordinary and fine. She shrugged and walked home.

The next morning, Ariadne sat at the kitchen table finishing her breakfast. She had decided the cure wasn't working. How could it work in such small doses? She wanted to feel something, something BIG. She'd sipped and sipped and so far all she'd felt was dizzy. The pharmacist was being overly cautious.

She uncapped the vial. It was still almost two thirds full. The heart spun lazily in a circle, then came to a stop, floating like a tiny purple raft in the liquid. She raised the vial to her lips and took a big swallow. Intoxicating! So clear and sweet it made her smile as she drank.

When she was done she noticed that everything looked very . . . attractive. The salt shaker on the table was attractive. The coffee in her cup was attractive. Her Cheery Os box had never looked so pretty before, nor had the spoon in her bowl ever seemed so appealing. She caressed the stem of the spoon and it arched to meet her fingertip. Ariadne gasped.

Impulsively, she grabbed the Cheery Os box and crushed it to her breast. She thrust back her chair, stood up, and began waltzing the cereal box round and around the kitchen. She knocked magnets off the refrigerator and a saucepan off the stove. She bumped the hanging plants, making them twirl on their macrame cords. She laughed, and kept spinning, cradling her dance partner in her arms.

In mid-whirl, she sensed that her comb wanted

her. She put down the Cheery Os box with some reluctance, then hurried into the bathroom. Yes! There it was on the shelf over the sink, her little black comb, its teeth strong and slender. She picked it up and felt the comb bite gently into her scalp at the part.

Ariadne shivered.

It eased downwards, teasing loose the tangles of her long, difficult dark hair.

Ariadne sighed.

The comb stroked faster and faster until Ariadne's hair crackled with electricity, shooting off sparks that lit up the bathroom. "Darling!" the comb cried. It swooned and dropped from her hand.

Much later, hours or days, maybe weeks later, Ariadne came to, sitting at the kitchen table. She was exhausted. The vial of medicine was in front of her, empty; even the purple heart was gone.

"Wow," she said.

She went back to the drugstore, of course. She wanted hundreds of those beautiful purple hearts. The pharmacist looked surprised when she walked in.

"Didn't expect to see you again so soon," he said in a friendly voice.

"I'd like more," she said, placing the empty vial in the middle of the counter top.

The pharmacist picked up the vial. He studied the label, shot a look at Ariadne, then read the label again. He scratched the top of his big head.

Ariadne shifted from one foot to the other. "Well?" she said.

"This prescription is for one time only," he said.

She looked at him, alarmed, then read the label for herself.

"Sips," he said, waggling his finger at Ariadne. "I told you to take sips."

Ariadne walked out of the drugstore and stood at the curb. Cars flew by, stirring up dust. The sun struggled to get out from behind a cloud. "This is humiliating," she said loudly. "Why do I have to buy my abandon? Why can't I do it on my own?"

The imperious orange hand, palm face-out, told her she couldn't cross the street yet. "Oh, shut up!" she said to it. "Don't tell me what to do! I'm tired of waiting."

She crossed the street, ignoring the curses of drivers and the squeal of their brakes. She was thinking hard about the bright yellow box tucked away in her cupboard and the little black comb that languished on her bathroom shelf.

"There has to be a way to recapture that feeling," she said to herself as she walked home. "Maybe if I touch the box in a certain way . . . maybe if I tell the comb how I really feel . . ." She walked faster, her heart quickening in her breast.

ARIADNE
TAKES
A BATH

Beleaguered by days and days of moodiness, Ariadne checked the calendar that hung on a string from the soap dish handle over the bathtub. It was a specially laminated calendar that her mother had given her for Christmas. Ariadne found that, yes indeed, once again she was premenstrual. She filled the tub and sank into the green-tinted water, submerging until her long hair floated like seaweed and only her face was dry. Then she remembered to take off her dress. She unzipped it and wiggled like a mermaid shedding her tail. The dress tangled between her feet. She kicked it across the room. It hit the bathroom wall with a splash and slid to the floor, defeated. Ariadne left her bra and underpants on because she felt mad at somebody. She didn't know who.

ARIADNE TALKS TO JESUS

Ariadne received a letter from Jesus. He asked about her cat. He wrote, "Are you taking good care of her? How about her fleas?" He enclosed a picture: a big circle and a little circle with whiskers and ears and a tail. Looked like a kid drew it. He wrote, "You may have guessed this already but my mother Mary is reincarnated in your cat. So please take good care of her. Love, Jesus."

After much thought Ariadne sent a postcard back to Jesus. "Dear Jesus," she wrote. "Your mother is doing fine. She sometimes scratches the oriental rug and she goes through a lot of expensive cat food but she is a sweet person. I am glad to take care of her." Ariadne drew him a picture of the Virgin Mary. She left out the halo, unsure of Mary's status in this life. This reminded her to ask: "Has your mother stepped up or down, Jesus? I have great respect for her as my cat, but she can't say much, can she?"

Jesus left a message on her answering machine: "Jesus calling. I can't discuss The Divine Plan with you. Everything is unfolding as it should. Get her a cat toy for Christmas, okay?"

Ariadne sat at her kitchen table drinking coffee, her third cup, and watched her cat eat Special Care cat food. She took a sip of coffee and wished that she could see The Divine Plan. She imagined it as a lengthy document, brilliant in its simplicity, and that when she read the outline for her life she would shout "Of course!" and the scales would fall from her eyes. She wondered why it was such a big secret. She wondered why Jesus couldn't take care of his own mother. Was he allergic to cat fur?

After many days she called Jesus. The line was busy the first three times she tried. Finally she got through and waited patiently as the phone rang and rang. He picked up and said, "Yes?"

Ariadne said, "There's someone here wants to talk to you."

"Oh, really?"

"Yes, really." And before he could hang up Ariadne put the receiver up to her cat's head, who happened to be looking out the window next to the telephone at that moment. Ariadne could hear, "Hello? Hello?" faintly from the receiver. The cat stayed very cool, swiveling her head only slightly toward the voice on the phone, all the time keeping her eyes on a pigeon that was perched on a telephone wire outside.

"Mom? Is that you?"

The cat twitched her ear and looked over at Ariadne.

"Mom! I know what you're thinking and it's true. You got a bum deal. But I swear it's all written up in The Plan."

Ariadne narrowed her eyes and the cat's tail weaved a figure eight. They hung up.

Ariadne held up a cocktail dress for the cat to see.

"How about this one?" she asked.

The cat continued to lick her paw as she sat on the end of the ironing board. Her tail twitched.

"Mmmm . . . I see what you mean. Too many sequins." A stack of books on reincarnation teetered on the other end of the ironing board. Ariadne had had a revelation. If her cat was the Virgin Mary then wasn't it possible that she, Ariadne, was the reincarnation of Mary Magdalene? She had been up all night writing a new plan. She called it Divine Plan #2.

The cat put on a beret, tilting it over one ear, and Ariadne put on a red silk cocktail dress. The two Marys were stepping out.

ARIADNE
HAS
DINNER

Ariadne stared down at the tangled mess of noodles on her plate. Long, flat noodles, hopelessly intertwined. Snakes. An orgy of thin white bodies. This wouldn't do.

"Straighten out!" she said. "Behave!"

"Make me," they said.

She sputtered at this audacity. She began the arduous task of straightening them out. She envisioned them in parallel lines, one fettuccini beside the next, no one touching their neighbor. But instead they slithered from her fork, they slid off the table, they snickered at her vision. She began to stab at them, regretting that she'd coated them with butter, back when they were innocent and fresh from the boiling pot. She managed to pinion one of them to the table-cloth and stretched it out to its full length. It quivered under her fingers. She began to feel triumphant; then she looked back at the glistening noodles that twisted on her plate.

She could see no other solution: she picked them up one by one and swallowed them. They went down slick and easy and straight as an arrow, from her lips to her throat to her stomach. She bypassed the chewing.

She was nearly done eating when she noticed her left arm writhing off to one side of her body. Then her foot began to rotate at the ankle with the toe pointed. Her hips rose of their own accord and swung from the left to the right. Her long hair lifted from her head and swayed like grass in a field. Then her breasts began to set a rhythm like a pair of maracas and she moved, sinuous and slow, across the room.

"Stop that!" she said to her limbs. "Straighten out!" she shouted at her breasts. "Everyone behave!"

"Make me," they said.

ARIADNE'S ARMOR

Ariadne bought herself a suit of armor from a junk shop on the corner. The knees were knobby and the helmet had a plume of ostrich feathers. Stiff leather gloves were attached at the ends of the metal arms. The shop owner had demonstrated how the top half detached from the bottom at the waist. And the helmet, of course, was re-movable. Ariadne thought she might slay a few fat dragons, free some distressed damsels from their chains, and be home in time to feed the cat.

The very next morning she sprang out of

bed to try on the armor. It stood in the corner looking dauntless and so sincere. Not being sure what people wore underneath their armor, Ariadne opted for a plain white tank top and underpants. She wrapped her arms around the suit and dragged it over beside a kitchen chair. Getting into the armor would be a challenge; the legs were so rigid she couldn't possibly climb in from a standing position without hurting herself. So instead she laid the bottom half on the floor and wiggled her body across the linoleum and into the cavernous metal legs. Then, grabbing hold of the kitchen chair she dragged herself upright and took some deep breaths. She was delighted to discover that the breastplate opened on hinges, like a door, making it easier to insinuate her arms into the top half. Her fingers curled slightly, conforming to the shape of the gloves.

But the helmet, oh, the helmet was a marvelous experience. Ariadne peered at her kitchen through vertical slits in the visor. She was very, very far inside the armor, secure and alone. And because of this, the room looked very, very bright and interesting. She saw painted-red chairs, an ivy draped over and around a window, a squat container of blue dishwashing liquid. Her breath pulled in and out, whistling softly inside the helmet. "Hello," she said to her cat, and laughed because she'd deepened her voice without thinking about it. She knocked on her chest; how massive she was!

Her mother, coincidentally, was knocking on her door at the same time. Ariadne let her in. Her mother looked frail; her legs and arms were like sticks, and her white hair seemed thinner than before. Ariadne offered a metal elbow for her mother to cling to as they crossed the room to the kitchen table. She noticed that her mother hesitated before sitting down; the seat of the chair was a little dusty.

"Wait!" She bent over, sweeping the ostrich feathers on the top of her helmet back and forth over the surface of the chair. They sat down to have orange pekoe tea and Pop Up Tarts together. After the boiling water had been poured over their tea bags, the lemon squeezed and the sugar swirled, after Ariadne's visor had creaked open and shut several times to allow for drinking, her mother asked her if she was having a nice day.

"Yes," Ariadne said, "Very."

Her mother nodded and said that was nice.

Ariadne leaned back in her chair. It shifted under the extra weight of the armor. She leaned forward again and rested her elbows in between the tea things. "And you?" she asked. "Are you having a nice day?"

"Yes," her mother said. "I'm having a very nice day."

Ariadne tried to cross her legs, but the armor made that impossible. She drew a squiggly pattern in a drop of spilled tea. "Would you care for another tart?" she asked.

Her mother said that she enjoyed Pop Up Tarts, particularly the strawberry kind, but that she was full. "Thank you anyway," she said.

"I almost got blueberry."

"Oh, really?" her mother said. "What made you change your mind?"

"Strawberry just seemed nicer," Ariadne said.

They took final sips of their tea in silence and returned the cups to their saucers. Her mother smiled and patted Ariadne's gloved hand. "I must be going, dear." She stood, clutching the edge of the table to keep her balance.

Ariadne stood, too, rattling the tea cups and knocking over her chair. Her feet made a hollow, clanking sound as she walked her mother to the door.

"See you next week?" she asked.

"Yes," her mother answered.

FORGETFUL

Ariadne remembered to breathe on Sunday. As dusk fell, painting the horizon a mustard yellow and party dress pink, she stood on her fire escape watching. The iron slats of the fire escape pressed into the soft rubber bottoms of her sneakers. Suddenly, her lungs hitched and a squeak escaped from her nose. She took great gasps of delicious air; her knees wobbled; her lungs swelled like grateful balloons.

"Oh, my," she said, leaning back against the wrought-iron railing. "This is different."

ARIADNE GOES TO THE GROCERY STORE

The fluorescent lighting at Spendid Foods hurt Ariadne's eyes. And then there were all the bright colors of the products, especially in the cereal aisle. Red and yellow made her feel out of control. She kept forgetting things and had to backtrack for chocolate chips.

The check-out lines were long, but she managed to queue up at Annie's register. Annie was tall. Annie had sweet brown eyes. Annie was kind to all of her customers, treating their bananas and apples with respect.

As Ariadne watched Annie talk in a personal way with each shopper, she longed to touch the cashier's curly brown hair. She wanted to tousle it and feel the shape of Annie's skull beneath her hand. Ariadne tipped her own head back and forth, imagining a hand ruffling and caressing. "Aaahh," Ariadne said out loud and a small boy turned around and stared at her. Ariadne smiled and put a divider down behind the boy's mother's groceries.

The black conveyor slipped past, always in the direction of Annie. Ariadne placed her hands lightly over the conveyor and felt the rubber glide beneath her palms. The woman shopper who was behind her in line cleared her throat. Ariadne sighed. She took her package of chocolate chips out of her cart and smacked it down onto the conveyor. The shiny yellow bag rode gaily to the end of the belt and was stopped by Annie's hand.

"Hi," Annie said.

Ariadne took off her shoes. She unbuttoned her wool coat and laid it in her cart on top of her groceries. Then she grasped the edge of the check-out counter with both hands and hoisted herself up onto one knee. Her jeans restricted her movement a little but she managed to lie down comfortably on the conveyor belt, her head towards Annie. The belt skidded under her calves and butt, up her spine and bumped her head out onto the scanner.

"Hey!" said the woman shopper next in line.

Ariadne looked up into the eyes of Annie the cashier with the hands that never bruised your fruit and said, "Hi."

A KNOCK
AT THE DOOR

The pillow was flat again. Ariadne plumped and persuaded, but it remained unwelcoming. The orange numbers of her digital clock on the bedside table said 3:02 3:02 3:02. She got up. She opened the window, shivered, closed it, opened it a crack, then got back in bed.

There came a knock at the front door.

Ariadne put on an over-sized, long sleeved red shirt. She felt her way through the dark to the living room and stood fearfully, not sure what was real. The knock came again, louder, rattling the door on its hinges. She opened the door quickly.

A man stood in the lighted hallway, wearing a business suit and carrying a briefcase. His eyes were hidden by reflective sunglasses. He showed her a plastic-encased card that said FBI. He wasted no time. He asked, "What is your relationship with women?"

Ariadne twisted a button on her shirt.

"Women?" she said. "Women can be close, and it's perfectly natural." She paused. "Don't you think?"

The FBI man said nothing. He set his briefcase down on the hall floor. He snapped it open, took out an ink pad and a rubber stamp with a shiny black handle.

Ariadne watched him and felt confused. The wallpaper was garish in the hallway, orange as a Crayola crayon. How had she not noticed this before?

"I'm not sure what you mean by relationship," she said. "Maybe if you gave me a definition of the word, I could answer you better. I relate to some people more than others, and sometimes I relate to certain women more than other women. But that doesn't mean I relate exclusively to a certain woman. Or at least, that's never happened before."

In the silvery lenses of the FBI man's sunglasses, Ariadne saw the reflection of the bare lightbulb hanging overhead. She watched as he balanced his rectangular pad on a raised knee and pressed the rubber stamp down firmly into the ink.

"Is this the kind of thing you wanted to know?" Ariadne asked. "Because I'm innocent of whatever you're suggesting. Sometimes I can't even decide where to kiss a woman . . . the lips or the cheek? So I veer at the last minute and kiss her beside the nose. An odd, nowhere sort of place—not the lips, not the cheek, not even the forehead. It's awkward, but it's the best I can do."

The FBI man frowned. He got a clean rag out of his briefcase. He fastidiously wiped the rubber stamp clean, then once again pressed its face into the ink.

"I haven't been sleeping well," Ariadne confided. "I had this dream. I'm flying low over a city at night. I'm wearing a pink feather boa. My toes are pointed. What am I supposed to do with my arms? I try to look it up in a flight manual, but the pages keep flipping by in the wind and the words are in some foreign language. I'm losing altitude. The feather boa gets tangled around my legs. In desperation, I say 'I'm not afraid! I'm not afraid! I'm not afraid!' and somehow this keeps me from falling out of the sky."

Ariadne looked hard at the FBI man. "What do you think of that?" she said.

The FBI man would not meet her eyes. He seemed to be deep in thought, or maybe he was just inspecting the stamp to see if it was inked properly.

Ariadne was getting a little pissed off. The hall light was bright and her feet were cold. "I just love them, okay? Is that what you want to hear? I love women. Now go away and let me sleep."

He seized her wrist. Ariadne shouted, "No!" and yanked her hand away. They grappled with each other, the lightbulb swinging wildly on its cord above their heads. The stamp flashed; Ariadne shoved and kicked to avoid its imprint. In unison, they both let go. Ariadne clutched her hands to her breast, panting from the struggle, but triumphant.

The FBI man repacked his briefcase, then stood up and straightened his tie. "It is our policy," he said, "to shoot down unidentified flying objects."

He turned sharply on his heel and left.

ARIADNE'S EGG

Ariadne put her soul in the freezer.

The freezer was old, white, and scratched around the handle; humming loudly, it took up half the space in a small back room in Ariadne's apartment. The freezer light came on when she lifted the heavy lid, and her cat sprang up onto the lip and balanced herself there. They looked in at frozen loafs of pumpernickel bread, a frost-covered box of ice cream, fat little chickens, a plastic bag of peas.

Ariadne took out her soul and placed it in the freezer beside the ice cream. Her soul looked like an ostrich egg, but it was soft and warm and vibrated when you touched it.

This was one of those rare occasions when Ariadne's cat disapproved.

Ariadne ignored the cat, saying, "You're always so serious. I'm just trying a little experiment." She closed the lid, shooing her cat out of the way.

She went to the cellar and did her laundry. She didn't think about it during the washing or drying cycles. But as she folded the fresh-smelling sheets and separated her warm socks and underpants into piles on the table, a wave of sorrow swept through her.

"What the hell did I do?" She hurried back upstairs.

Her soul was still there, an over-sized egg nestled beside the ice cream. She was surprised to see that it was already coated with a thin layer of frost.

"Back where you belong," she said, lifting it up, then lowering it down onto the crown of her head. It bumped against her skull, bruising it, but her soul wouldn't go back in.

"Oh, stupid!" said Ariadne, starting to panic. "It's frozen solid!" She looked around anxiously for a warm place to set it down.

The next day Ariadne sat on her couch. It was late afternoon, but the shades were still drawn. She wore yesterday's shirt and jeans, very wrinkled, and one of yesterday's socks was on the foot propped on the coffee table. Her other foot, which was bare, stirred up dust balls on the floor.

A saucer full of stubbed-out cigarettes was perched on the arm of the couch by her elbow. She'd developed a terrible craving that morning and had run out to the corner store where she'd looked at candy bars, packages of cookies, bottles of wine. She'd settled on a pack of cigarettes. Now she searched through the butts in the saucer, licking her dry lips and squinting as bits of ash swirled up into her eye. The cat jumped up onto the back of the couch to watch her.

"What do *you* want?" she said. The cat didn't answer.

Her soul sat beside her on the middle cushion of the couch. To avoid looking at it, she re-lit one of the squashed cigarettes and stood up. She sucked at the cigarette fiercely, pacing the room, raking the fingers of her free hand through her hair. Finally, she stopped in front of the egg and stared at it.

All night long she'd tried to get it back into her body. With numb fingers, she'd held it against her head, then her chest, her stomach, the small of her back. Feeling foolish, she'd even sat on it. Nothing worked. Her soul knocked against her body, but wouldn't enter.

She bent down and spoke loudly to the egg, as if it were deaf. "Hey! I am sick of this!" She nudged it with a fingertip; it wasn't soft, it wasn't warm, and it didn't vibrate.

"I should have bought some cookies, too." Her cat continued to stare at her from the back of the sofa.

"Okay!" Ariadne said to the cat. "I made a mistake! Now just shut up about it." She stubbed out her cigarette and looked hopefully for another one inside the empty pack on the floor. Nothing. Disgusted, she sat down on the coffee table in front of her soul. It glowed in the darkening room. She leaned over, resting her forehead against its round surface. "God," she said. "I hate myself."

She climbed onto the sofa, lay on her side, and wrapped herself around the cold egg. Shivering, she reached for an afghan and a pillow.

Ariadne fell asleep. She dreamed that her soul had turned into a peach: dark orange, yellow, a stripe of delicate pink. It didn't look like her soul, but she knew that it was. She brushed it lightly against her cheek.

Someone was behind her. A hand slid under her

hair and stroked the back of her neck. A chin rested on Ariadne's shoulder. "Bite it," said a woman's soft voice in her ear.

"Oh! Right!" Ariadne said, surprised she hadn't thought of this herself. She ate the bright flesh of the peach, sucking the juice, licking her sticky fingers. By the time she had exposed the dark rippled pit, she was flushed and warm.

"This is *really* good," Ariadne said. "Who would have guessed that my soul was delicious?"

The someone behind her laughed, and pressed closer. The laughter spiraled in Ariadne's body. She felt strong arms encircling her waist, gentle hands caressing her breasts.

"Sweet Jesus," she whispered, and awoke.

ARIADNE GOES GROCERY SHOPPING AGAIN

Anxiety attacked Ariadne in the footcare section of the grocery store. Beige-colored pads hung from hooks in the wall: callus removers, arch supporters, toe cradlers, heel cushioners. Shouldn't toenail clippers be here somewhere? She felt the movement of shoppers steering their carts around her, little gusts of displaced air. She also felt their sense of purpose, knew they had long lists clutched in their hands, knew that they saw her as an indecisive twig in the middle of their stream.

She had a list, too. It said:

lemon

dill

clippers

The bunch of dill lolled in the front corner of the cart and the lemon rolled about, its color startling and unreal. She wandered toward the dentalcare section (were teeth related to toenails?) and endured the overwhelming sight of boxes and boxes of toothpaste stacked in perfect alignment. She felt the panic rise into her chest. She thought she might shriek if she didn't find the toenail clippers soon.

There was a green thread lying on the gray linoleum floor. She reached down and picked up the end of it: dental floss, mint-flavored, waxed. The length of thread tightened as she lifted it and she saw, much to her surprise, that it extended down the entire length of the aisle and around the corner. It vibrated, taut as a bow string, tight as a fishing line, a whisper-thin umbilical cord stretching from her fingertips to whatever waited on the other end.

Abandoning the dill, the lemon and the search for the toenail clippers, she walked away from her cart and followed the floss. It wound around the corner (she avoided toppling a chinaware display), down the length of the garbage bag aisle, twisted its way between a freestanding freezer of ground turkey and a pile of plastic pitchers and ice cube trays, then led her on a straightaway past the fresh cod packed in ever-falling crushed ice. A little old man with a big head, wearing a leather vest and a purple tie, watched her go by. It was her pharmicist! He gave her a secretive wave, his hand held close to his waist. She smiled at him and kept following the green thread.

She entered the fruit and vegetable area; the thread stretched up and over a display of honeydew melons, luminous as a pile of moons.

"Jesus!" said Ariadne. She thought about going around but decided that would be cheating. Keeping tight hold of the thread with her left hand she clambered amidst the melons. The roundnesses were delightful and she was sorry to leave them behind as she topped the display and climbed headfirst down into the angularity of bananas.

The other shoppers remained calm, deciding perhaps that the safest course was to act like Ariadne was a TV show. They watched with their mouths slightly agape.

She disentangled herself from the bananas and began to follow the thread at a feverish pace, breaking into a trot to keep up with the rhythm of her reaching hands. As she passed the checkout counters she waved to Annie the cashier that never bruised your fruit, who waved back, smiling, but Ariadne didn't stop. The baking supplies aisle flashed by: brown sugar, white sugar, cubed sugar, salt. Just ahead she saw a woman leaning her shoulder against the paper-wrapped packages of flour. The thread was trapped against the shelves by the woman's body. Ariadne came to a full stop.

"Excuse me, I need to get by."

The woman, who had a glorious head of short lively red hair (why do they call it red, Ariadne wondered, it's deep orange) straightened up but didn't move out of the way. She was tall with strong shoulders, dressed in a green short-sleeved shirt and tea-colored cordoroys.

"I'm Harriet," she said.

"I'm in a hurry," Ariadne said.

The Harriet person said, "I need to find the feet stuff. These damn boots make my arches ache and they squash my little toe." She gestured down to her feet (the boots had bright green laces) and smiled winningly at Ariadne.

Ariadne blushed. She forgot the floss in her hands. "You look like a tree," she observed.

"Why, thank you," said Harriet.

ARIADNE
DOES
A LITTLE
GARDENING

Ariadne watered her only plant, a pink and green-leaved coleus that sat on her coffee table. She could smell spaghetti sauce drifting up from the downstairs apartment through the open windows. Outside, her street was under attack; a big machine was breaking up tar with a piston. The leaves of the coleus trembled with every thump. Ariadne sat down and massaged the spot between her eyes. She felt one of her headaches coming on.

The coleus was small and spindly. What the hell did it want? she wondered irritably.

Plant food? Closer to the window? A bigger pot? "I'm not a mind reader," she said to the plant. "You've got to tell me what you need."

Her headache got worse, pounding in a counter rhythm to the piston outside; tendrils and then roots of pain crept around inside her skull, behind her eyes, at the back of her neck. The spaghetti sauce from downstairs was nauseating—too much oregano—and the odor invaded her living room, clinging to her curtains, saturating her sofa. Ariadne pressed the sides of her head with her palms and moaned. It felt like something was trying to break out, a pressure building and building. A dime-sized segment of her skull crumbled like hard soil, and out of the very top shot a perfect coleus, pink and green, and GIGANTIC, like the plume on a showgirl's headdress.

"What a relief," Ariadne said to the little coleus on the coffee table. "I've been holding that in for a long time."

ARIADNE RIDES THE BUS

"Morning," she said to the bus driver. She offered her dollar and the machine sucked the money into its slotted mouth. Hard plastic seats the color of salmon lined either side of the aisle. A woman sat in her usual second seat back; she wore a battered beige coat and an inch of grey showed at the part in her otherwise black hair, like a secret she was slowly revealing. Ariadne sat a few seats behind her.

The bus pulled away. It maneuvered perilously close to cars, a graceful dinosaur dipping and swaying down the street. Ariadne loved that her seat was so high. The sidewalk skimmed by beneath her window. Sunlight flickered past telephone poles, touching her eyelids, making her smile.

Someone pulled the cord and the Stop Requested sign lit up at the front of the bus. A teenaged boy got off, then a skinny man wearing cowboy boots sprang up the steps with a Styrofoam cup of coffee in his hand. He sat behind the bus driver and talked about fishing like he did every Saturday. The bus pulled away from the curb.

Ariadne could hear a little boy singing a made-up song at the back of the bus. Now and then his mother would shush him. A college girl sat across the aisle, marking up a book with a lime green highlighter. Bracelets clattered on her wrist when she turned a page.

The bus swung over to the curb and Ariadne looked to see who was getting on. When she saw, her heart left her body and flew around the inside of the bus three times before returning to her chest. It was Harriet the Tree.

She climbed on the bus, looking lithe and leggy. The wind had played rough with her short red hair. She dropped a handful of change into the machine without counting it, clapped the bus driver on the shoulder and shouted a greeting to Mr. Cowboy Boots.

Harriet apparently didn't notice Ariadne because she sat down behind the old woman. Immediately, Harriet leaned forward and asked her a question. Ariadne heard something about "sore neck?" The old woman nodded and smiled and Harriet began to massage the woman's neck and shoulders. The old woman kept reaching back and patting Harriet's hand gratefully.

"Jeez!" Ariadne muttered. Her stomach felt weird.

Harriet got up and weaved with the movement of the bus down the aisle to the college girl. She sat in the seat in front of her, twisting around to talk. Ariadne felt invisible. She couldn't help but overhear their conversation.

"*Crime and Punishment*, huh?"

"Yah . . . I'm writing a paper."

"How many pages?"

"Too many. My hand aches."

"Let me see your hand." The girl offered up her slender arm and Harriet massaged her wrist, the base of her thumb, the fingertips. The bracelets clanked and jangled.

Ariadne rolled her eyes and looked out the window. "Cripes!" she said.

Harriet then left the girl and went to the back of the

bus. A few minutes later Harriet's husky voice joined with the little boy's in a made-up song about fish. It went: "Fish in the elevator! Fish in the elevator! Where are we going? Up, up, up! Fish in the elevator!"

Ariadne had heard enough. She yanked the overhead wire, the sign blinked on, the bus swerved to a stop. As she walked down the aisle everyone got quiet. At the top of the steps she gripped the railing with a sweaty hand. The bus driver swung the door open and glanced at her. "On or off, sister?" he said, not unkindly.

Her feet wouldn't move. The border of ads running along the upper wall of the bus looked down on her as she stood there, silently exhorting her to give plasma, to go to college, to watch the local news station. In short, to make up her mind.

"Ariadne!"

"Oh, shit," she whispered, and turned around. Her knees were trembling. Harriet stood in the aisle, her hands thrust into the pockets of her worn corduroys. The bus driver closed the door. He set the parking brake, switched on the emergency blinkers, and swiveled in his seat to watch. The old woman, the man with the cowboy boots, the college girl, the mother and her little boy: all of them watched as

Ariadne walked back to Harriet. She stopped within touching distance.

"I like your shirt," she said, staring at the pattern of overlapping leaves on Harriet's upper body.

Harriet smiled at her. "Thanks," she said.

"Are your feet feeling better?" Ariadne asked.

Harriet wiggled her bare toes, and Ariadne noticed for the first time that Harriet was wearing flip-flops. The thongs made bright blue Vs over the tops of her strong feet. "Much better," Harriet said, "They can breathe."

Ariadne looked out the window at the cars hesitating, then creeping, then surging foward. A car's horn beeped loudly three times. The passengers on the bus winced and hunched their shoulders up around their ears. Ariadne turned back to Harriet, and said, "I'd like you to touch *me*."

Harriet's gray eyes widened, then turned a darker shade of gray. She leaned forward, stepping right out of her flip-flops, and gripped the backs of the seats on either side of the aisle for balance.

"Where?" she asked.

Ariadne's lips tingled, her cheeks flushed, her nose buzzed. Her eyes brimmed with tears, which she tried to blink away.

64

"Here," she said, laying her hand over her stomach.

Harriet stepped closer and lifted the hem of Ariadne's shirt so she could see her belly button. It folded in sweetly, like the entrance to a tiny seashell. Harriet nodded and knelt on the floor of the bus, resting one hand on Ariadne's hip. She pressed her ear against the soft skin, listening, then turned her head to kiss, and kiss again.

Ariadne shivered. Her hand floated out, hovering near Harriet's shoulder. "Where is your stop?" she asked.

"I don't have one planned," said Harriet, smoothing Ariadne's shirt back into place.

"Me neither," said Ariadne. "I see no reason for stopping." Harriet got up from the floor and the two of them sat down together.

The little boy began to sing again; the college girl made a note in the margin of her book. The bus driver released the parking brake and turned off the emergency blinkers. He made sure everyone was seated, glanced in the sideview mirror, then eased them out into the exciting rush of traffic.

THE BELLY AQUARIUM

Ariadne became fascinated by pregnant bellies—skin stretched smooth like satin, belly buttons gaping, mysterious flutters under questioning hands. Everywhere she looked bellies rose to meet her like beachballs floating on a lake. The bellies lifted the front hems of dresses and nudged their way to the front of the line. They said "Look at me" or "Place your hand here" or "I'm much bigger than you'll ever be." Ariadne was charmed by this forwardness, and inspired.

So she grew one down in the cellar at night while everyone else in the world was sleeping.

This took considerable concentration and, yes, even faith to accomplish. Nevertheless she persisted, night after night creeping down the cellar stairs to the purple armchair abandoned in the corner, where she sat and sang to her stomach. Oh, how she sang! She sang for polliwogs to stir in the mud and open their eyes, for brilliant crayons to burst free of their boxes, for fragile young women to be acknowledged as poets, for stubble-faced fathers to weep in their coffee, for horses to gallop through patio doors. She sang and she sang until, night by night, she detected a fullness, a rising like firm bread dough left on the radiator.

She liked her new belly. The fishbabies multipled inside her: two and ten and then hundreds swimming in the belly aquarium. Plants grew up and a miniature castle materialized that the fishbabies played in when they were restless. A deep sea diver wearing a bubble helmet floated behind a treasure chest with a gold lock.

Occasionally one or two would slip out of Ariadne's mouth when she was talking. They'd dart into the air, scales flashing silver and blue, and slide into other people's pockets. She would say "Oh, do you mind?" and if people didn't mind they'd take one home. It didn't seem to matter what people did with their fishbaby—fry it up and eat it for supper, flush it down the toilet, wear it like an earring, start their own aquarium—just so long as they loved it a little bit.

Late one night, while she lay in her bed, Ariadne was visited by the spirit of her dead father. He sat in a chair close beside her. His hands were clasped together and hung between his knees, a weight that pulled his head forward and down. He wore a plaid wool shirt and wool pants with leather-lined pockets. She waited for him to speak, her own hands resting lightly on the curve of her celestial body.

"Unnatural," he said, his voice rumbling up through his heavy feet and legs, his bowed spine, his hunched shoulders.

The fishbabies swam into the heart of the castle and huddled together, waiting. Bubbles leaked from the sea diver's mouthpiece and floated in a silent line to the top of the belly aquarium.

Ariadne imagined spouting fish like a fountain, head back and mouth open, showering the room, burying the spirit of her dead father under her beloved babies.

Instead, she reached across the blankets and laid the back of her hand against his cheek. The stubble vibrated under her fingers. As she stroked the prickly jaw, the spirit of her dead father inclined his head and sighed deeply.

ARIADNE'S
BLIND SPOT

Ariadne was not kissing Harriet. They were sitting close together on Ariadne's sun-dappled bed, and she had been pondering this lack of kissing for the past ten minutes.

"Would you like some tea?" she asked uncertainly.

"No thanks," said Harriet.

Ariadne wondered if she'd overdressed for this date. She looked down at her strapless prom dress: layers of tulle, ranging in color from pale pink to the deepest rose prickled her bare knees. The satin bodice had stays that pressed into her ribs and prevented the dress from falling down. The stays (and the nearness of Harriet's hand next to hers on the bedspread) made it hard for her to breath.

What an idiot I am, she thought, glancing at Harriet's white shirt and jeans. Ariadne unlaced her stiff work boots and kicked them off, relieved that at least one part of her body could be comfortable.

"I could do that," said Harriet. Ariadne looked at her questioningly.

"I can massage your feet. I'm good at it."

"You want to?" Ariadne was a little embarrassed of her feet.

"I'd love to," said Harriet, momentarily blinding Ariadne with her smile.

Ariadne lay down on her bed, her dress rising up around her like a bell. She smoothed it down and surrendered her feet to Harriet.

"You have nice arches," said Harriet.

"Thanks," said Ariadne, who then fell silent, amazed by the things Harriet was doing down there. Harriet's fingers found the tender spots on her feet, then traveled upwards over the ankles to her calves, where she coaxed and cajoled the muscles until they gave in. It wasn't long before a moan escaped from Ariadne's lips.

A man with a gray crewcut drifted into the bedroom.

"Who the hell is that!?" said Harriet.

Ariadne sat up. "Oh, that's my father." She flipped the edge of the bedspread so it covered her legs. "He's been dead for a while."

Her father's spirit wandered around the room, never looking directly at Ariadne or Harriet. He looked under the bed, then noisily opened a desk drawer and peered in.

"What does he want?" said Harriet.

Ariadne watched him. He closed the drawer, then started picking up and putting down photographs on top of the desk. "He keeps losing things. This morning it was his cigars. Yesterday I think it was his pocket watch. He'll go in a minute."

Her dead father stopped fumbling around and went over to the window. He opened it and stepped out.

"Wow!" said Harriet. "He can fly?"

"No." Ariadne laughed. "He likes to go out on the fire escape."

Harriet frowned. "So he lives here?"

"Well, he doesn't *live* here," Ariadne said. "He's around."

Harriet found Ariadne's foot under the bedspread and brought it out again. She squeezed the heel in the palm of her hand. "Did you step on a clam shell once?"

"Where?"

"Right here." Harriet traced the half-moon scar on the little toe.

"Oh . . . yes. It really hurt."

She relaxed back into the pillow and watched Harriet gently knead her toes. Occasionally, one of the joints popped.

"Are you cold?" Harriet asked.

"Maybe a little. This dress is kind of drafty."

Harriet reached for the afghan at the bottom of the bed and covered Ariadne's bare shoulders with it. She lingered, awkwardly smoothing and tucking. "Better?" she asked.

Their eyes met, and Ariadne thought: Her lips will taste like peaches.

Her dead father ducked back through the open window. He sat on the windowsill and lit a cigar, blowing large smoke rings over the bed.

"Good! He found them," Ariadne said. "He must've left them in the flower pot out there."

The room filled with blue smoke. Harriet wrinkled her nose and gave Ariadne a pointed look.

"Just ignore him," Ariadne said. "He likes to be in on things."

72

"And you don't mind?" asked Harriet.

Ariadne considered. "I don't think about it much."

"Really?" Harriet said skeptically. She went back to Ariadne's feet, picking them up and holding them against her stomach. "Why don't you say, 'Spirit, be gone!'"

"It wouldn't work."

"How do you know? Have you tried?"

Ariadne struggled to her elbows, said, "Go away, Dad," and flopped back onto the pillow.

Her father studied the glowing tip of his cigar.

"That was half-hearted," said Harriet. "We need him out of here!"

"You deal with dead fathers your way, and I'll do it my way."

"Oh . . . I see," said Harriet, and resumed the massage, pressing both thumbs deeply into Ariadne's arch.

"Oww!"

"Sorry."

Ariadne's father got up from the windowsill and wandered about the room, puffing on his cigar. He read all the titles of the books in the bookshelf, then he came over to the bed and sat down with his back to Ariadne and Harriet. The bed springs complained and the mattress shifted.

"Oh my God," said Harriet.

Ariadne looked at her father's back, so close she could touch his scratchy wool shirt if she wanted to, then she looked at Harriet's face. "Maybe we should do this some other time." She slid her feet out of Harriet's hands and tucked them out of sight.

Harriet jumped up and faced Ariadne's father. "Get off! Ariadne, tell him!"

Ariadne looked helplessly at Harriet. "He doesn't mean any harm. You'll get used to him, I promise! Maybe if we do something else, he'll go back out on the fire escape."

"I don't want to do something else, God damn it!" Harriet kicked the bed frame and glared at the father. He blew a smoke ring which grew to the size of a hula hoop before it disappeared. "And neither do you!" she shouted at Ariadne. She left the bedroom, slamming the door behind her.

Ariadne winced. She and her father stared at the door for a long moment, then he got up and started opening desk drawers. The top drawer stuck, and he pulled at it doggedly, the wood grinding and the knob coming loose as he pulled.

"It's in your other hand, Dad," Ariadne said tiredly. She pointed to his smoking cigar. "It's right there in your hand. Can't you see it?"

ARIADNE IN THE BATHROOM AGAIN

A riadne was watching a commercial on television. A woman in a tasteful suit walked down a hallway, one hand clutching her stomach, her other hand pressed to the side of her head. A disembodied voice said, "Your period brings cramps, headaches, bloating, and irritibility. You're not yourself."

Ariadne flicked the television off.

"I'm not myself," she said.

Her arms tingled and her hands felt heavy. She got up from the couch and shook them, doing a rag-doll dance, but they still felt like somebody else's arms. She took them with her when she went into the bathroom to take a bubble bath. As she waited for the bubbles to rise she paced in agitated circles to the left, round and round the edge of the shaggy pink carpet. The pink rosebuds in the vinyl wallpaper winked at her; the fuzzy pink toilet seat cover brushed against her calf as she passed. Her arms swung at her sides and her hands bumped random articles to the floor: the soap dish, seashells, an African violet, the cat.

Because her lower back hurt atrociously she realized that she hated the tasseled lamp shade on the wall fixture. She raised her right hand to eye level, pointed her forefinger and shot the lamp shade off the wall. It flew in an arc across the room, a bright pink bird with a hole torn in its side, and fluttered down to rest in the bathwater. It bobbed rhythmically, half-submerged in the foam. The silence after the shot was so domestic, so friendly, Ariadne felt betrayed.

"I'm *rarely* myself," she told the stupid-looking palm plant on the back of the toilet. "In fact," she said to the empty-headed loofahs rimming the bathtub, "I'm so rarely myself, I think I might become this other person full-time." She looked down at her hand, cautiously, and saw that the tip of her forefinger was smoking.

"Huh," she said.

She sat down on the toilet seat and leaned over the bathtub. The lamp shade floated in the water, its tassel-hair limp and tangled. Ariadne pressed its pink side and it flipped over, exposing splayed wire circles that dipped in and out of the foam. The moisture made her fingertip sputter and hiss. I've killed it, she thought.

"Why didn't you defend yourself?" she asked the lamp shade peevishly. "You knew I was coming in here."

The lamp shade was unable to answer. Ariadne didn't feel like taking a bubble bath anymore.

ARIADNE WALKS ON THE MOON

Ariadne walked across the moon's surface. The sky above was very black, a big black bowl. For some reason the gravity was making her feel heavier, rather than lighter. She dragged her feet through the moon dust, leaving parallel tracks like a cross-country skier. She wore her pea green raincoat with all the buttons snapped and the hood pulled up.

Nearby she saw a tiny crater, like a dry wading-pool, and three old women were sitting around the edge with their feet on the crater floor. Ariadne could hear them talking as she trudged towards them; their voices had a bell-like quality in the moon's atmosphere. She stopped and surveyed the moonscape. Empty craters dimpled the surface in every direction.

She stood only ten feet away from the women now, but since none of the three looked at her, she started to circle their little crater. Ariadne thought they looked like nice old women, dressed in their terrycloth slippers, their stretch slacks, their floral polyester blouses. They rested their elbows on a card table and joked and squabbled as they played cards, cheating if the opportunity came, but admitting it cheerfully if they were caught.

Ariadne walked close enough to peek over a woman's shoulder. This particular woman had freshly permed blue-white hair and Ariadne could smell the cloying aroma of beauty salon products. The woman had a good hand for gin rummy: three queens and two jacks. Ariadne thought about making an encouraging comment, but didn't want to ruin the game. No one acknowledged her. She turned away.

There were thousands of other craters to choose from, so she trudged to another wading-pool–sized one nearby. She climbed down into the crater, which wasn't very deep, and stood in the center of it. She took off her sneakers and socks. Her bare feet sank into the moon dust while she arched her lower back against her palms. She didn't bother to take off her raincoat.

"It's not worth the trouble," she said to herself.

"Gin!" one of the card players called out. There were groans and sighs, then the sound of shuffling and the sharp flick of card sliding over card for the deal.

Ariadne lay down in the dust. She looked up through the opening of her raincoat's hood and saw an oval of black sky. The stars were chinks of light piercing the blackness. She felt an object lodged under her right shoulder and pulled it out.

"Is that an eight or a three?" asked one of the old women to the cardplayer beside her. There was a silence, then the second woman said, "A nine."

The object was an old-fashioned black rotary telephone. Ariadne rested it on her chest and dialed Harriet's number.

"Hi, it's me," she said.

"Why haven't you called?" said Harriet, her voice rough with worry. "Where are you?"

"Well . . . it's a long-distance call," said Ariadne.

"How long a distance?"

Ariadne rolled her head to one side and looked at the blue planet slowly spinning in the night sky. She wanted to dive into that coolness, that blueness, and be revived. A single tear wandered from the corner of her eye and mingled with her hair. "I can't seem to get back," she said.

"Are you alone?" Harriet asked.

Ariadne listened to the old women's voices spiraling in the dark air.

"Yes," she said.

"Don't move. I'm coming to get you."

Ariadne wondered about this for a moment, then said, "Really? I'm no good at giving directions."

Harriet said, "Don't worry. I can find you."

Ariadne felt a little blur of hope as she hung up the phone. She struggled to sit up, then leaned back on her hands. The old women were taking a break from their card game. They were eating vanilla sandwich cookies and drinking apple cider out of transparent plastic cups. Ariadne felt a thirst that no amount of cider could satisfy.

Then she saw a dot of orange moving on the far side of the moon. The dot came striding towards her in a straight line, and soon she recognized the dot as Harriet's hair, vibrant against the gray moonscape. Harriet was carrying a huge watering can, the weight pulling one shoulder down. She walked right up to the edge of Ariadne's crater and looked in. They both smiled.

"Thanks for coming," Ariadne said.

Harriet tipped the watering can and watered Ariadne's bare feet. Ariadne shuddered and tried to avoid the stream pouring out of the spout. Harriet persisted and began to water Ariadne's legs.

"Yuck," said Ariadne.

Harriet said, "Take off your raincoat, honey. You're going to have to get wet."

Reluctantly, Ariadne removed her pea-green raincoat. Underneath it, she was wearing a beautiful body. She squeezed her eyes shut and received a gush of water on the crown of her head.

"Oh, Lord," she said, snuffling to keep it out of her nose. It flowed like a waterfall, splashing over her shoulders, streaming between her breasts, pooling in the cups of her upturned hands. Finally, she opened her mouth and drank.

When the little crater was more than halfway full Harriet threw down the watering can and climbed in beside Ariadne, who was soaking up water like a moon cactus. Harriet reached out her hand and slowly followed the slippery path of Ariadne's long dark hair down into the niche of her neck and out over the curve of her shoulder. They touched forehead to forehead and leaned into each other, gently rocking, until waves lapped the shores of their tiny moon crater.

ARIADNE JOINS THE CIRCUS

Ariadne looked down. Hundreds of faces, their features blurred by the bright lights in the circus tent, looked up at her. She balanced lightly on the edge of the tiny platform and tried to breathe. Her heart fluttered in her chest. The green-and-white-striped tent arched overhead, while far below a huge barrel of water waited for her. She wasn't as high up as the trapeze act, but she was higher than the elephants, higher than the giraffe they brought out once a show and paraded around the inner ring. She was far above the hoops that were set aflame for the Fabulous

Fifi to jump through. "That dog is so brave," she said to herself as she scanned the crowd. She didn't see Harriet.

"Guess she couldn't make it," Ariadne said, and tried not to feel too disappointed.

She liked her diving costume: a midnight-blue leotard, blue tights, and a blue bathing cap to restrain her difficult dark hair. She looked down again, past the pointed toes of her silver diving slippers to the barrel of water directly below.

"The first time is always the hardest," she said, encouraging herself. Slowly, she raised her arms over her head and bent her knees, readying herself for the dive.

An expectant murmur rose from the crowd. Ariadne noticed something odd. She looked over one shoulder at the people below and behind her, then over the other shoulder. She lowered her arms and turned in a circle, checking every face in every seat under the Big Top.

"How curious!" she said. "They're all women."

Women cracked peanut shells open and licked the salty insides; women in pairs sucked soda from jumbo cups passed back and forth between them; women sat on their tail bones with their knees wedged against the seat in front of them; women wore baseball caps backwards and chewed gum; women held bunches of balloons and women nibbled at pink cotton candy; women told jokes and women laughed at jokes; women fanned their faces with programs; women jumped up to go to the bathroom. Several pointed up at Ariadne on her platform, then traced her route down through the air to the huge barrel of water in the center ring. They wanted to see some action.

Ariadne was at first charmed by this audience (a surge of electricity went up her spine), but then she began to feel afraid. She was an amateur. She would let them down.

"The sword swallower!" she yelled to them. "The lion tamer, or the tightrope walker! They're the ones you want to see!"

A babble of discontent rose from the bleachers. A few women booed. Popcorn and peanuts began to fly through the air. "Try a Jackknife!" someone called. "A Triple Gainer!" another suggested.

A high, teasing voice cried, "Don't worry, honey, we'll catch you!" Laughter surrounded this last remark. Ariadne angrily snatched the blue bathing cap from her head and threw it in the direction of the voices. Her hair tumbled down around her shoulders.

"You try it!" she shouted. "You climb that wobbly rope ladder and stand up here all by yourself!"

The women in the audience talked to each other. Ariadne could see their heads shaking yes and no, their hands gesturing in the semi-darkness. Then several women spoke, their eager voices overlapping:

"We're sorry . . ."

"We can't help ourselves . . ."

"This is big . . ."

"We're so excited!"

The teasing voice broke in, shouting: "What do you expect? We've been waiting forever!"

Ariadne folded her arms over her breast and scowled. "There's no safety net! I'll take as long as I want to!"

Soothing voices came from every section of the tent. "We know! . . . Yes . . . Don't worry . . . You can do it!"

"As if they could catch me," Ariadne muttered fiercely. "What a joke!"

She stepped forward again and looked down. The water in the barrel was black. The barrel itself didn't seem very big any more; the sandy floor of the center ring, however, looked immense.

"Oh, God!" she moaned, clutching her head in her

hands. "How could I be so naive? I might die!"

Silence filled the tent. Every woman contemplated Ariadne's fate. The odds were not in her favor.

"You might get lucky," a clear, low voice said.

Ariadne shaded her eyes against the bright lights. Who had said that? In the back row, near the main entrance, a tall woman was standing. She was in the shadows, but still . . . was that a glint of red in her hair? Was the body strong and straight like a tree? Ariadne couldn't be sure.

"Harriet?" she said softly.

A different woman stood up, this one in the middle row. "I agree," she said sweetly. "You might get lucky."

A third woman, wearing sweat pants and a T-shirt, stood. "Yes," she said, and Ariadne recognized her teasing voice from earlier. "You might indeed get lucky."

Women were standing up all around the tent now, and Ariadne heard the word "lucky . . . lucky . . . lucky" spoken by a hundred different overlapping voices. She blinked in astonishment and turned round and around on the platform. The women's faces glowed beneath her. They looked so beautiful, so familiar . . . as if she'd known them all her life. And Harriet was out there, if not inside the tent, then somewhere near.

"I'm going to jump," she said, and was surprised to hear herself say this. She wiped the sweat from her palms onto her tights. Her legs were shaking.

"I don't have to do this well," she told herself. "I don't have to be fast, or smooth, or impress anyone." The women quieted down; the word "lucky" was spoken by ten, and then five, and then by a single voice which faded to nothing.

"I just have to do it," Ariadne whispered into the silence. She backed up a few paces and took a deep breath. A dog barked somewhere backstage.

"Fabulous Fifi," she said, and smiled. She closed her hands into fists. She planted the ball of her left foot firmly behind her. The platform seemed to be floating, the bright edge in front of her cutting the darkness.

"Okay," she said. "Now." She ran one, two, three steps and launched herself out into space.

ARIADNE
AND
HARRIET

Ariadne stood on her fire escape. Trees glittered with ice under the streetlights. She leaned forward against the wrought-iron railing and watched two people with identical pom-poms on their wooly hats hurry down the street. Their arms were linked and their laughter tinkled like the icy branches of the trees in the wind. Ariadne shifted her slippered feet to keep them warm; she pulled her plaid flannel bathrobe closer to her body, retying the cloth belt in a half bow.

"Jeez Louise, it's cold out here!" she said, shivering, looking up at the fierce little stars in the sky. She heard the window open behind her. There was the chink of a boot, then the other boot, stepping out onto the iron slats of the fire escape.

"Are you crazy? Where's your coat?"

Ariadne smiled without turning from the railing. A footstep. Then she felt the warm surprise of Harriet's breasts against her back and the weight of Harriet's extra-large leather jacket folding around her shoulders. She looked down and watched Harriet's hands slowly zip them both into the one jacket, enclosing them in soft leather and sheepskin.

"I wanted to feel the cold," she murmured, leaning back.

Harriet nuzzled Ariadne's hair, breathing in deeply. "Why?"

"Because I can laugh at the cold if I know that you're here."

Ariadne's cat miaowed from the open window. She jumped down and circled them, rubbing against their legs with such fervor she almost lost her balance.

"Hey!" said Ariadne. "I was wondering when you'd show up."

They looked at the shining black trees, the snow on the railing, the abundant bright stars. It was quiet, except for the sound of the cat's purr.

90

"He's not here," said Harriet softly.

"Not here," Ariadne agreed. "Not tonight."

"Good."

Ariadne laughed. "Yes." She twisted her body around within the jacket to find Harriet's lips. "Good."

ARIADNE HAS A SMALL WEDDING

The empty sanctuary smelled of musty hymnals and dead flower arrangements and cocoa. Ariadne walked down the center aisle towards the altar. She wore overall shorts with black leggings and a black turtleneck with holes in the elbows. The floorboards under the padded carpet creaked. With her hands in her pockets, she started doing a step-together-step-together-step, keeping time with the creaks. On the altar was a gold cross and a sky-blue mug with steam rising out of it, spiraling up into the spaces of the Gothic ceiling. Ariadne focused her eyes on the steam spiral as she made her procession down the aisle.

Each of the three steps made a chirping sound under her feet as she climbed to the altar. She picked up the mug from beside the cross and looked inside: minature marshmallows floated in dark, rich cocoa. She raised the cup to her lips and blew softly, making the marshmallows bob and crowd to the far edge. The scent of chocolate made her smile. She sipped.

The spirit of her father rose from the seventh pew back. His plaid wool shirt looked too hot for the time of the year and his crew cut had grown too long on top.

Ariadne looked out over the broad curve of pews toward the back of the church, where the shadows were deepest. Her mother was there; she held a white wedding dress in her arms. The pearls sewn into the fabric of the dress glowed like fireflies in the dim light. Her mother lifted the dress up and down on its hanger, smiling at Ariadne; the fireflies became agitated. Ariadne grimaced, put down her cocoa, and stuck her hands deep into her overall pockets.

Her father's spirit called out from his pew, "It would make your mother happy!" He seemed startled by the sound of his own voice and sat down.

Ariadne saw that her mother was now waving a

bouquet of yellow daylilies in the air.

"Oh, you are too much," Ariadne said, exasperated. "This is not going to happen that way!"

Her father's spirit stood up again, ran a pale hand through his overgrown crew cut and said, "Your mother will be disappointed."

Ariadne walked back and forth in front of the altar. She stopped, took a sip of the cocoa to calm her nerves, put it back down beside the cross, and began to speak.

"I have brought myself here today to join myself together in holy matrimony. It has come to my attention that I am split into many pieces, scattered about like birdseed on the ground, and although this is interesting, it is also disturbing." She paused.

"If there is anyone here that knows a reason why I shouldn't come together today, speak now or forever hold your peace." She walked to the edge of the steps, put her hands on her hips, and glowered at her parents. Her father's spirit started to speak, coughed, then picked up a hymnal and began flipping through the pages.

"Onward Christian Soldiers," he read. "A Mighty Fortress is Our God."

Ariadne shook her head. "Those aren't reasons, Dad."

94

Her mother became frantic at the back of the church, wringing her hands, close to tears. Fear boiled its way down the aisle, threatening to scald Ariadne where she stood.

"Oh, Mom . . . no," Ariadne said as she sidestepped the emotion. "That's not a reason either."

She sat down on the top step and clasped her hands around her knees. Her boots looked up at her, round-toed and friendly. She addressed her boots as she spoke, because it seemed appropriate.

"I, Ariadne, take myself, Ariadne, to be my thanks-giving cactus, my carousel horse, my frost heave, my doorbell, my Cheery Os box. I take myself breathing, I take myself dead, I take the witch living inside of my head. For richer, for poorer, in good times and bad, I make myself take myself, just as I am."

Ariadne glanced up. "What God has brought together let no one split asunder."

The pew haunted by her dead father was empty. The entire church was empty. She retrieved her cup from the altar, sat down again on the top step, and drank the last of the warm cocoa in one long swallow. The marshmallows were melted and luscious.

"I now pronounce myself married," she said softly, and kissed herself twice on each knee.

 CHRYSTAL WING lives in Portland, Maine. She received a B.S. in Music Education from the University of Southern Maine in 1980, and taught music at Waynflete School in Portland for the next ten years. She began her writing career in 1990 and completed her MFA in Writing at Goddard College in Plainfield, Vermont in 1995. Her affiliation with Godard college continues, as a founding member of the Clockhouse Writers Conference, an annual alumni gathering, held on the campus each summer. She now teaches creative writing for Portland Adult Education, in the gifted, talented programs in middle schools for the Portland School District, and at several retirement homes. Some of her short work has appeared in *The Dissident* and *Utidy Candles*. *Ariadne's Egg* is her first published book, and Chrystal is at work on a subsequent volume, *Ariadne and Harriet*.

LEZLI MORGAN, cover painting artist, lives in the Pacific Northwest. Her work has been displayed in one person and group exhibits, in Ketchikan, Juneau, Anchorage and Seattle. She received the category award for painting in the 1996 and 2000 All Alaska Juried Art Exhibition. "Luna" 1995, oil and copper leaf on linen, belongs to the private collection of Molly McCafferty. The Luna Moth is found only in North America. It is considered an endangered species due to pollutants and pesticides. While also a play on words, the artist says, "Luna" is about longing for the unattainable. More of Lezli's paintings are available for viewing at www.lezlimorgan.com.

		DATE DUE	
JUN 0 3 2003			
JUL 2 4 2003			
AUG 2 6 2003			
OCT 0 7 2003			
DEC 1 2 2003			
JAN 0 2 2004			
AUG 1 7 2006			
DEC 0 4 2007			